A Fish Out Of Water

By Helen Palmer

Illustrated by P. D. Eastman

COLLINS

I CAN READ IT ALL BY MYSELF

Beginner Books

Trademark of Random House, Inc., William Collins Sons & Co. Ltd., Authorised User

3 4 5 6 7 8 9 10

ISBN 0 00 171307 8 (paperback)
ISBN 0 00 171114 8 (hardback)

A Beginner Book published by arrangement with
Random House, Inc., New York, New York
First published in Great Britain 1963

Printed in Great Britain by
William Collins Sons & Co Ltd, Glasgow

"This little fish,"
I said to Mr. Carp,
"I want him.
I like him.
And he likes me.
I will call him Otto."

"Very well," said Mr. Carp.
"Now I will tell you
how to feed him."

Then Mr. Carp told me:
"When you feed a fish,

never feed him a lot.
So much and no more!
Never more than a spot,
or something may happen!
You never know what."

Then I took Otto home.

I gave him some food.

I did not give him much.

Just one little spot!

But this did not make Otto happy.

He wanted more food.

He had to have more.

Poor Otto!

He just HAD to have more!

I knew what Mr. Carp
had told me:
"Never feed him a lot.
Never more than a spot!
Or something may happen.
You never know what."
But I gave Otto all the food
in the box.

Then something DID happen.

My little Otto began to grow.

I saw him grow.

I saw him grow and grow.

Soon he was too big

for his little fish bowl.

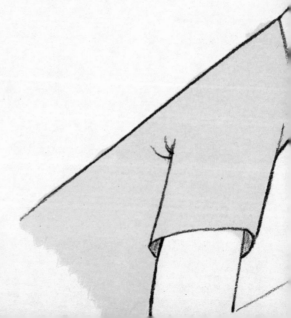

There was just one thing to do.

I put Otto into the flower bowl.

"There, Otto," I said.

"This will hold you."

But, no!

The flower bowl did not hold him.

Otto went right on growing!

This was not funny.

Not funny at all!

His tail was growing

right out of the top.

I grabbed the flower bowl.

I ran with it.

"Otto," I said,

"I know just where to put you.

Then you will be all right."

I put him in a big pan.

But Otto was not all right.

I saw him grow some more.

Very soon he was too big

for the pan.

I put him in pan after pan.

He was growing so fast.

Poor Otto!

My poor little fish!

Oh, why did I feed him so much?

"Otto," I said,

"stop growing! Please!"

But Otto could not stop growing.

He was growing all the time.

Very soon I ran out of pans.

Otto had to have water.

There was just one thing to do.

I did it.

I grabbed him.

I grabbed him by the tail.

I ran with him.

Up to the bath!

The bath is big.

It can hold lots of water.

At last!

"There, Otto," I said.

"This bath holds my father.

This bath holds my mother.

So, it will hold you."

But the bath did not
hold him at all.
He went right on growing.
"Oh, Otto," I said,
"what can I do now?"

Then — crash!

The door went down.

Crash!

Otto went down.

I went down, too.

Oh, what a ride!

Down went the water
into the cellar.
And down went Otto, too.
I had to do something fast.
I grabbed the phone.

I called a policeman.

"Help! Help!" I said.

"I fed my fish too much.

Mr. Carp told me not to.

But I did!"

"What?" said the policeman.
"Mr. Carp told you not to
but you did? Too bad!
I will come at once."

The policeman came.

"My fish went that way," I said.

"He is down in the cellar."

The policeman ran down with me.

"What a fish!" he said.

"He is much too big to

keep in a cellar.

We will have to get him out."

We had to work and work
to get Otto out.
Poor Otto!
Oh, why did I feed him too much?
Mr. Carp told me
something would happen.
And it did. It did!

Now we had Otto out of the cellar.
But now Otto had no water.
No water at all!

"A fish has to have water,"
I said to the policeman.
"We must take him to water.
Get help!
Call for help on the radio."

The policeman called on the radio.

He called for the firemen.

"Help! Help!" he said.

"A boy has fed a fish too much!"

"A boy has fed a fish too much?
We will come at once."

The firemen came.

They all helped to get Otto up.

"But where can we take him?"

I asked. "Up town? Down town?"

"To the pool!"

yelled the firemen.

"To the pool!"

I yelled.

"And please hurry!"

They did hurry.
The fire engine with Otto
came right up to the pool.
The firemen yelled,
"Every one get out of the pool!
This fish is going in."

Down into the pool went Otto.

Into the pool

with a big, big splash!

Now I was happy.

Now, at last, my Otto had water.

Lots of water!

This big pool was just the thing.

This big pool would hold him.

But Otto went right on growing.
And no one wanted Otto in the pool.
They did not like Otto at all.
"You take that fish out of here!"
they yelled.

There was just one thing to do.

I did it. I ran to the phone.

I called Mr. Carp.

"Please, please help me!" I said.

"I fed Otto too much."

"Oh, dear!" said Mr. Carp.

"So you fed him too much!

I knew you would.

I always say 'don't'

but you boys always do.

Yes, I will come."

Then Mr. Carp came.

He had a black box in his hand.

He had a lot of other things, too.

"What are you going to do, Mr. Carp?"

I asked him.

But Mr. Carp said nothing.

He just went right up to the pool.

He took his black box with him
and all the other things, too.
SPLASH!
Mr. Carp jumped into the pool.

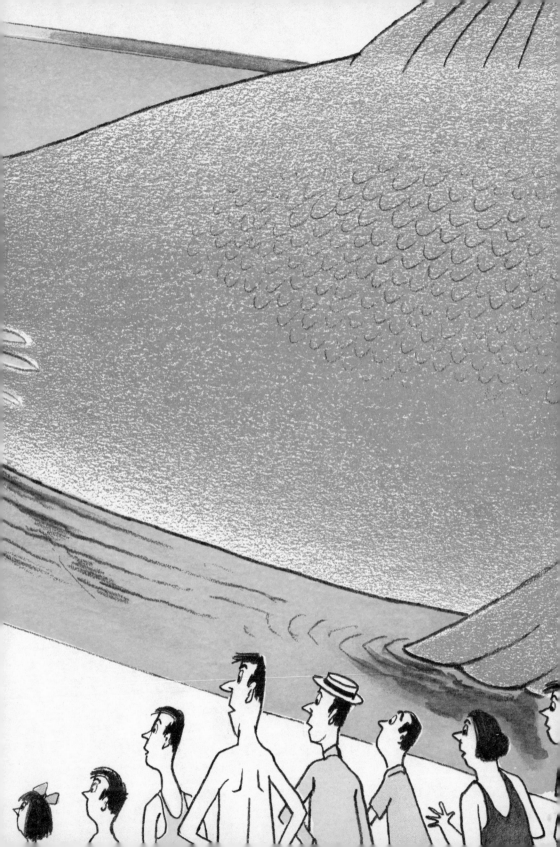

SPLASH!

Now Otto went down, too!

All I could see was his tail.

I could not see Mr. Carp at all.

What was going on down there?

What were they doing down

there in the water?

Now I could see nothing.
Not Otto.
Not Mr. Carp.
Nothing at all.
Would I see my Otto again?
Would I see Mr. Carp again?

"Mr. Carp, Mr. Carp!"
I yelled. "What are you doing?
Are you all right?"

Then up jumped Mr. Carp.

In his hand was a little fish bowl.

In the bowl was my Otto!

Mr. Carp had made him little again.

"Don't ask me how I did it," he said.

"But here is your fish."

"And from now on," said Mr. Carp,
"PLEASE don't feed him too much.
Just so much, and no more!"

Now that is what I always do.

Now I feed Otto

so much and no more.

Never more than a spot

or something may happen.

And now I know what!